PENGUIN PLAYS

THE LAST YANKEE

Arthur Miller was born in New York City in 1915 and studied at the University of Michigan. His plays include *All My Sons* (1947), *Death of a Salesman* (1949), *The Crucible* (1953), *A View from the Bridge* and *A Memory of Two Mondays* (1955), *After the Fall* (1963), *Incident at Vichy* (1964), *The Price* (1968), *The Creation of the World and Other Business* (1972), and *The American Clock* (1980). He has also written two novels, *Focus* (1945) and *The Misfits*, which was filmed in 1960, and the text for *In Russia* (1969), *Chinese Encounters* (1979), and *In the Country* (1977), three books of photographs by his wife, Inge Morath. His most recent works are *Salesman in Beijing* (1984), *Danger: Memory! Two Plays* (1987), *Timebends*, a memoir (1988), *The Ride Down Mt. Morgan* (1991), and *Broken Glass* (1993), both plays. He has twice won the New York Drama Critics Circle Award, and in 1949 he was awarded the Pulitzer Prize.

BY ARTHUR MILLER

DRAMA

The Golden Years
The Man Who Had All the Luck
All My Sons
Death of a Salesman
An Enemy of the People (*adaptation of the play by Ibsen*)
The Crucible
A View from the Bridge
After the Fall
Incident at Vichy
The Price
The American Clock
The Creation of the World and Other Business
The Archbishop's Ceiling
The Ride Down Mt. Morgan
Broken Glass

ONE-ACT PLAYS

A View from the Bridge, *one-act version, with* A Memory of Two Mondays
Elegy for a Lady (*in* Two-Way Mirror)
Some Kind of Love Story (*in* Two-Way Mirror)
I Can't Remember Anything (*in* Danger: Memory!)
Clara (*in* Danger: Memory!)

OTHER WORKS

Situation Normal
The Misfits (*a cinema novel*)
Focus (*a novel*)
I Don't Need You Anymore (*short stories*)
Theatre Essays
Chinese Encounters (*reportage with Inge Morath photographs*)
In the Country (*reportage with Inge Morath photographs*)
In Russia (*reportage with Inge Morath photographs*)
Salesman in Beijing (*a memoir*)
Timebends (*autobiography*)

COLLECTIONS

Arthur Miller's Collected Plays (Volumes I and II)
The Portable Arthur Miller
The Theater Essays of Arthur Miller (*Robert Martin, editor*)

VIKING CRITICAL LIBRARY EDITIONS

Death of a Salesman (*edited by Gerald Weales*)
The Crucible (*edited by Gerald Weales*)

TELEVISION

Playing for Time

SCREENPLAYS

The Misfits
Everybody Wins
The Crucible

The Last Yankee

With a new essay
About Theatre Language

ARTHUR MILLER

PENGUIN BOOKS

PENGUIN BOOKS
Published by the Penguin Group
Penguin Books USA Inc., 375 Hudson Street,
New York, New York 10014, U.S.A.
Penguin Books Ltd, 27 Wrights Lane, London W8 5TZ, England
Penguin Books Australia Ltd, Ringwood, Victoria, Australia
Penguin Books Canada Ltd, 10 Alcorn Avenue,
Toronto, Ontario, Canada M4V 3B2
Penguin Books (N.Z.) Ltd, 182–190 Wairau Road,
Auckland 10, New Zealand

Penguin Books Ltd, Registered Offices:
Harmondsworth, Middlesex, England

First published in Great Britain by Methuen Drama,
an imprint of Reed Consumer Books Ltd. 1993
This edition with a new essay by Arthur Miller
published in Penguin Books 1994

1 3 5 7 9 10 8 6 4 2

LIBRARY OF CONGRESS CATALOGING IN PUBLICATION DATA
Miller, Arthur.
The last Yankee: with a new essay, about theatre language/
Arthur Miller.
p.   cm.
ISBN 0 14 048.151 6
1. Psychiatric hospital patients—United States—Drama.
2. Mentally ill women—United States—Drama.   3. Marriage—United
States—Drama.   I. Title.
PS3525.I5156L37   1994
812'.52—dc20   93-20950

Printed in the United States of America
Set in Bembo

To Inge Morath

CONTENTS

The Last Yankee   1

      A Note on the Play   3

      Cast of Characters   5

About Theatre Language   75

The Last Yankee

A NOTE ON THE PLAY

The Last Yankee received its premiere at the Manhattan Theatre Club, New York, on January 21, 1993, with the following cast:

Leroy Hamilton	John Heard
John Frick	Tom Aldredge
Patricia Hamilton	Frances Conroy
Karen Frick	Rose Gregorio
Unnamed Patient	Charlotte Maier

Directed by John Tillinger
Set design by John Lee Beatty
Costume design by Jane Greenwood
Lighting design by Dennis Parichy
Sound design by Scott Lehrer

The play received its British premiere at the Young Vic Theatre, London, on January 26, 1993, with the following cast:

Leory Hamilton	Peter Davison
John Frick	David Healy
Patricia Hamilton	Zoë Wanamaker
Karen Frick	Helen Burns

Directed by David Thacker
Set design by Sheilagh Keegan
Costume design by Helen Skillicorn
Lighting design by Jim Simmons
Movement by Lesley Hutchinson

CAST OF CHARACTERS

Leroy Hamilton
John Frick
Patricia Hamilton
Karen Frick
Unnamed patient

SCENE ONE

The visiting room of a state mental hospital. Leroy Hamilton is seated on one of the half-dozen chairs, idly leafing through an old magazine. He is forty-eight, trim, dressed in subdued Ivy League jacket and slacks and shined brogans. A banjo case rests against his chair.

Mr. Frick enters. He is sixty, solid, in a business suit. He carries a small valise. He looks about, glances at Leroy, just barely nods, and sits ten feet away. He looks at his watch, then impatiently at the room. Leroy goes on leafing through the magazine.

FRICK, *pointing right:* Supposed to notify somebody in there?

LEROY, *indicating left:* Did you give your name to the attendant?

FRICK: Yes. 'Seem to be paying much attention, though.

LEROY: They know you're here, then. He calls through to the ward. *Returns to his magazine.*

FRICK, *slight pause:* Tremendous parking space down there. 'They need that for?

LEROY: Well a lot of people visit on weekends. Fills up pretty much.

FRICK: Really? That whole area?

LEROY: Pretty much.

FRICK: 'Doubt that. *He goes to the window and looks out. Pause.* Beautifully landscaped, got to say that for it.

LEROY: Yes, it's a very nice place.

FRICK: 'See them walking around out there it's hard to tell. 'Stopped one to ask directions and only realized when he stuck out his finger and pointed at my nose.

LEROY: Heh-heh.

FRICK: Quite a shock. Sitting there reading some thick book and crazy as a coot. You'd never know. *He sits in another chair. Leroy returns to the magazine. He studies Leroy.* Is it your wife?

LEROY: Yes.

FRICK: I've got mine in there too.

LEROY: Uh, huh. *He stares ahead, politely refraining from the magazine.*

FRICK: My name's Frick.

LEROY: Hi. I'm Hamilton.

FRICK: Gladameetu. *Slight pause.* How do you find it here?

LEROY: I guess they do a good job.

FRICK: Surprisingly well kept for a state institution.

LEROY: Oh, ya.

FRICK: Awful lot of colored, though, ain't there?

LEROY: Quite a few, ya.

FRICK: Yours been in long?

LEROY: Going on seven weeks now.

FRICK: They give you any idea when she can get out?

LEROY: Oh, I could take her out now, but I won't for a couple weeks.

FRICK: Why's that?

LEROY: Well this is her third time.

FRICK: 'Don't say.

LEROY: I'd like them to be a little more sure before I take her out again. . . . Although you can never *be* sure.

FRICK: That fairly common? —that they have to come back?

LEROY: About a third they say. This your first time, I guess.

FRICK: I just brought her in last Tuesday. I certainly hope she doesn't have to stay long. They ever say what's wrong with her?

LEROY: She's a depressive.

FRICK: Really. That's what they say about mine. Just gets . . . sort of sad?

LEROY: It's more like . . . frightened.

FRICK: Sounds just like mine. Got so she wouldn't even leave the house.

LEROY: That's right.

FRICK: Oh, yours too?

LEROY: Ya, she wouldn't go out. Not if she could help it, anyway.

FRICK: She ever hear sounds?

LEROY: She used to. Like a loud humming.

FRICK: Same thing! Ts. What do you know! —How old is she?

LEROY: She's forty-four.

FRICK: Is that all! I had an idea it had something to do with getting old . . .

LEROY: I don't think so. My wife is still—I wouldn't say a raving beauty, but she's still . . . a pretty winsome woman. They're usually sick a long time before you realize it, you know. I just never realized it.

FRICK: Mine never showed any signs at all. Just a nice, quiet kind of a woman. Always slept well . . .

LEROY: Well mine sleeps well too.

FRICK: Really?

LEROY: Lot of them love to sleep. I found that out. She'd take naps every afternoon. Longer and longer.

FRICK: Mine too. But then about six, eight months ago she got nervous about keeping the doors locked. And then the windows. I had to air-condition the whole house. I finally had to do the shopping, she just wouldn't go out.

LEROY: Oh I've done the shopping for twenty years.

FRICK: You don't say!

LEROY: Well you just never think of it as a sickness. I like to ski, for instance, or ice skating . . . she'd never come along. Or swimming in the summer. I always took the kids alone . . .

FRICK: Oh you have children.

LEROY: Yes. Seven.

FRICK: Seven!—I've been wondering if it was because she never had any.

LEROY: No, that's not it. —You don't have *any*?

FRICK: No. We kept putting it off, and then it got too late, and first thing you know . . . it's just too late.

LEROY: For a while there I thought maybe she had too *many* children . . .

FRICK: Well I don't have any, so . . .

LEROY: Yeah, I guess that's not it either.

Slight pause.

FRICK: I just can't figure it out. There's no bills; we're very well fixed; she's got a beautiful home. . . . There's really

not a trouble in the world. Although, God knows, maybe
that's the trouble . . .

LEROY: Oh no, I got plenty of bills and it didn't help mine.
I don't think it's how many bills you have.

FRICK: What do you think it is, then?

LEROY: Don't ask me, I don't know.

FRICK: When she started locking up everything I thought
maybe it's these Negroes, you know? There's an awful lot
of fear around; all this crime.

LEROY: I don't think so. My wife was afraid before there
were any Negroes. I mean, around.

FRICK: Well one thing came out of it —I finally learned
how to make coffee. And mine's better than hers was. It's
an awful sensation, though —coming home and there's
nobody there.

LEROY: How'd you like to come home and there's seven of
them there?

FRICK: I guess I'm lucky at that.

LEROY: Well, I am too. They're wonderful kids.

FRICK: They still very young?

LEROY: Five to nineteen. But they all pitch in. Everything's clean, house runs like a ship.

FRICK: You're lucky to have good children these days. —I guess we're both lucky.

LEROY: That's the only way to look at it. Start feeling sorry for yourself, that's when you're in trouble.

FRICK: Awfully hard to avoid sometimes.

LEROY: You can't give in to it though. Like tonight—I was so disgusted I just laid down and . . . I was ready to throw in the chips. But then I got up and washed my face, put on the clothes, and here I am. After all, she can't help it either, who you going to blame?

FRICK: It's a mystery—a woman with everything she could possibly want. I don't care what happens to the country, there's nothing could ever hurt her anymore. Suddenly, out of nowhere, she's terrified! . . . She lost all her optimism. Yours do that? Lose her optimism?

LEROY: Mine was never very optimistic. She's Swedish.

FRICK: Oh. Mine certainly was. Whatever deal I was in, couldn't wait till I got home to talk about it. Real estate, stock market, always interested. All of a sudden, no interest whatsoever. Might as well be talking to that wall over there. —Your wife have brothers and sisters?

LEROY: Quite a few, ya.

FRICK: Really. I even thought maybe it's that she was an only child, and if she had brothers and sisters to talk to . . .

LEROY: Oh no—at least I don't think so. It could be even worse.

FRICK: They don't help, huh?

LEROY: They *think* they're helping. Come around saying it's a disgrace for their sister to be in a public institution. That's the kind of help. So I said, "Well, I'm the public!"

FRICK: Sure! —It's a perfectly nice place.

LEROY: They want her in the Rogers Pavilion.

FRICK: Rogers! —that's a couple of hundred dollars a day minimum . . .

LEROY: Well if I had that kind of money I wouldn't mind, but . . .

FRICK: No-no, don't you do it. I could afford it, but what are we paying taxes for?

LEROY: So they can go around saying their sister's in the Rogers Pavilion, that's all.

FRICK: Out of the question. That's fifty thousand dollars a year. Plus tips. I'm sure you have to tip them there.

LEROY: Besides, it's eighty miles there and back, I could never get to see her . . .

FRICK: If they're so sensitive you ought to tell *them* to pay for it. That'd shut them up, I bet.

LEROY: Well no—they've offered to pay part. Most of it, in fact.

FRICK: Whyn't you do it, then?

LEROY, *holding a secret:* I didn't think it's a good place for her.

FRICK: Why?—if they'd pay for it? It's one of the top places in the country. Some very rich people go there.

LEROY: I know.

FRICK: And the top doctors, you know. And they order whatever they want to eat. I went up there to look it over; no question about it, it's absolutely first-class, much better than this place. You should take them up on it.

LEROY: I'd rather have her here.

FRICK: Well I admire your attitude. You don't see that kind of pride anymore.

LEROY: It's not pride, exactly.

FRICK: Never mind, it's a great thing, keep it up. Everybody's got the gimmes, it's destroying the country. Had a man in a few weeks ago to put in a new showerhead. Nothing to it. Screw off the old one and screw on the new one. Seventeen dollars an hour!

LEROY: Yeah, well. *Gets up, unable to remain seated.* Everybody's got to live, I guess.

FRICK: I take my hat off to you—that kind of independence. Don't happen to be with Colonial Trust, do you?

LEROY: No.

FRICK: There was something familiar about you. What line are you in?

LEROY, *he is at the window now, staring out. Slight pause.* Carpenter.

FRICK, *taken aback:* Don't say. . . . Contractor?

LEROY: No. Just carpenter. —I take on one or two fellas when I have to, but I work alone most of the time.

FRICK: I'd never have guessed it.

LEROY: Well that's what I do. *Looks at his watch, wanting escape.*

FRICK: I mean your whole . . . your way of dressing and everything.

LEROY: Why? Just ordinary clothes.

FRICK: No, you look like a college man.

LEROY: Most of them have long hair, don't they?

FRICK: The way college men used to look. I've spent thirty years around carpenters, that's why it surprised me. You know Frick Supply, don't you?

LEROY: Oh ya. I've bought quite a lot of wood from Frick.

FRICK: I sold out about five years ago . . .

LEROY: I know. I used to see you around there.

FRICK: You did? Why didn't you mention it?

LEROY, *shrugs.* Just didn't.

FRICK: You say Anthony?

LEROY: No, Hamilton. Leroy.

FRICK, *points at him.* Hey now! Of course! There was a big article about you in the *Herald* a couple of years ago. Descended from Alexander Hamilton.

LEROY: That's right.

FRICK: Sure! No wonder! *Holding out his palm as to a photo.* Now that I visualize you in overalls, I think I recognize you. In fact, you were out in the yard loading plywood the morning that article came out. My bookkeeper pointed you out through the window. It's those clothes —if I'd seen you in overalls I'd've recognized you right off. Well, what do you know? *The air of condescension plus wonder.* Amazing thing what clothes'll do, isn't it. — Keeping busy?

LEROY: I get work.

FRICK: What are you fellas charging now?

LEROY: I get seventeen an hour.

FRICK: Good for you.

LEROY: I hate asking that much, but even so I just about make it.

FRICK: Shouldn't feel that way; if they'll pay it, grab it.

LEROY: Well ya, but it's still a lot of money. —My head's still back there thirty years ago.

FRICK: What are you working on now?

LEROY: I'm renovating a colonial near Waverly. I just finished over in Belleville. The Presbyterian church.

FRICK: Did you do *that*?

LEROY: Yeah, just finished Wednesday.

FRICK: That's a beautiful job. You're a good man. Where'd they get that altar?

LEROY: I built that.

FRICK: That altar?

LEROY: Uh huh.

FRICK: Hell, that's first-class! Huh! You must be doing all right.

LEROY: Just keeping ahead of it.

FRICK, *slight pause:* How'd it happen?

LEROY: What's that?

FRICK: Well coming out of an old family like that—how do you come to being a carpenter?

LEROY: Just . . . liked it.

FRICK: Father a carpenter?

LEROY: No.

FRICK: What was your father?

LEROY: Lawyer.

FRICK: Why didn't you?

LEROY: Just too dumb, I guess.

FRICK: Couldn't buckle down to the books, huh?

LEROY: I guess not.

FRICK: Your father should've taken you in hand.

LEROY, *sits with magazine, opening it:* He didn't like the law
either.

FRICK: Even so. —Many of the family still around?

LEROY: Well my mother, and two brothers.

FRICK: No, I mean of the Hamiltons.

LEROY: Well they're Hamiltons.

FRICK: I know, but I mean— some of them must be pretty
important people.

LEROY: I wouldn't know. I never kept track of them.

FRICK: You should. Probably some of them must be pretty big. —Never even looked them up?

LEROY: Nope.

FRICK: You realize the importance of Alexander Hamilton, don't you?

LEROY: I know about him, more or less.

FRICK: More or less! He was one of the most important Founding Fathers.

LEROY: I guess so, ya.

FRICK: You read about him, didn't you?

LEROY: Well sure . . . I read about him.

FRICK: Well didn't your father talk about him?

LEROY: Some. But he didn't care for him much.

FRICK: Didn't care for *Alexander Hamilton*?

LEROY: It was something to do with his philosophy. But I never kept up with the whole thing.

FRICK, *laughing, shaking his head:* Boy, you're quite a character, aren't you.

*Leroy is silent, reddening. Frick continues chuckling
at him for a moment.*

LEROY: I hope to God your wife is cured, Mr. Frick, I hope
she never has to come back here again.

FRICK, *sensing the hostility:* What have I said?

LEROY: This is the third time in two years for mine, and I
don't mean to be argumentative, but it's got me right at
the end of my rope. For all I know I'm in line for this
funny farm myself by now, but I have to tell you that this
could be what's driving so many people crazy.

FRICK: What is!

LEROY: This.

FRICK: This what?

LEROY: This whole kind of conversation.

FRICK: Why? What's wrong with it?

LEROY: Well never mind.

FRICK: I don't know what you're talking about.

LEROY: Well what's it going to be, equality or what kind
of country —I mean, am I supposed to be ashamed I'm
a carpenter?

FRICK: Who said you . . . ?

LEROY: Then why do you talk like this to a man? One minute my altar is terrific and the next minute I'm some kind of shit bucket.

LEROY: Hey now, wait a minute . . . !

LEROY: I don't mean anything against you personally, I know you're a successful man and more power to you, but this whole type of conversation about my clothes— should I be ashamed I'm a carpenter? I mean everybody's talking "labor, labor," how much labor's getting; well if it's so great to be labor how come nobody wants to be it? I mean you ever hear a parent going around saying— *mimes thumb pridefully tucked into suspenders*—"My son is a carpenter"? Do you? Do you ever hear people brag about a bricklayer? I don't know what you are but I'm only a dumb swamp Yankee, but . . . *Suddenly breaks off with a shameful laugh.* Excuse me. I'm really sorry. But you come back here two-three more times and you're liable to start talking the way you were never brought up to. *Opens magazine.*

FRICK: I don't understand what you're so hot about.

LEROY, *looks up from the magazine. Seems to start to explain, then sighs:* Nothing.

He returns to his magazine. Frick shakes his head with a certain condescension, then goes back to the window and looks out.

FRICK: It's one hell of a parking lot, you have to say that for it.

They sit for a long moment in silence, each in his own thoughts.

Blackout.

Most of the stage is occupied by Patricia's bedroom. In one of the beds a fully clothed woman lies motionless with one arm over her eyes. She will not move throughout the scene.

Outside this bedroom is a corner of the Recreation Room, bare but for a few scattered chairs.

Presently . . . from just offstage the sound of a Ping-Pong game. The ball comes bouncing into the Recreation Room area and Patricia Hamilton enters chasing it. She captures it and with a sigh of boredom goes offstage with it.

We hear two or three pings and the ball comes onstage again with Patricia Hamilton after it. She starts to return to the game offstage but halts, looks at the ball in her hand, and to someone offstage . . .

PATRICIA: Why are we doing this? Come let's talk, I hate these games.

Mrs. Karen Frick enters. She is in her sixties, very thin, eyeglasses, wispy hair.

I said I'm quitting.

Karen stares at the paddle.

Well never mind. *Studies her watch.* You're very good.

KAREN: My sister-in-law taught me. She used to be a stew-
ardess on the *Queen Mary*. She could even play when the
ship was rocking. But she never married.

PATRICIA: Here, put it down, dear.

*Karen passively gives up the paddle, then stands
there looking uncomfortable.*

I'm going to lie down; sit with me, if you like.

KAREN, *indicates Ping-Pong area:* Hardly anyone ever seems
to come out there.

PATRICIA: They don't like exercise, they're too depressed.

*Patricia lies down. The woman in the other bed does
not stir and no attention is paid to her.*

Don't feel obliged to say anything if you . . .

KAREN: I get sick to my stomach just looking at a boat.
Does your husband hunt?

PATRICIA: Sit down. Relax yourself. You don't have to talk. although I think you're doing a little better than yesterday.

KAREN: Oh, I like talking with you. *Explaining herself timorously; indicating offstage—and very privately* . . . I should go out—he doesn't like being kept waiting, don't y'know.

PATRICIA: Why are you so afraid? He might start treasuring you more if you make him wait a little. Come, sit.

> *Karen adventurously sits at the foot of the bed, glancing about nervously.*

Men are only big children, you know—give them a chocolate soda every day and pretty soon it doesn't mean a thing to them. *Looks at her watch again.* Only reason I'm nervous is that I can't decide whether to go home today. —But you mustn't mention it, will you?

KAREN: Mention . . . ?

PATRICIA: About my pills. I haven't told anybody yet.

> *Karen looks a bit blank.*

Well never mind.

KAREN: Oh! You mean not taking them.

PATRICIA: But you mustn't mention it, will you. The doctor would be very upset.

KAREN: And how long has it been?

PATRICIA: Twenty-one days today. It's the longest I've been clean in maybe fifteen years. I can hardly believe it.

KAREN: Are you Baptist?

PATRICIA: Baptist? No, we're more Methodist. But the church I'd really love hasn't been invented yet.

KAREN, *charmed, slavishly interested:* How would it be?

PATRICIA, *begins to describe it, breaks off.* I can't describe it. *A sign of lostness.* I was raised Lutheran, of course. —But I often go to the Marble Baptist Church on Route 91? I've gotten to like that minister. —You hear what I'm saying, don't you?

Karen looks at her nervously trying to remember.

I must say it's kind of relaxing talking to you, Karen, knowing that you probably won't remember too much. But you'll come out of it all right, you're just a little scared, aren't you. —But who isn't? *Slight pause.* Doctor Rockwell is not going to believe I'm doing better without medication but I really think something's clicked inside me. *A deep breath.* I even seem to be breathing easier. And I'm not feeling that sort of fuzziness in my head. —It's like some big bird has been hovering over me for fifteen years, and suddenly it's flown away.

KAREN: I can't stand dead animals, can you?

PATRICIA: Well just insist that he has to stop hunting! You don't have to stand for that, you're a *person*.

KAREN: Well you know, men like to . . .

PATRICIA: Not all—I've known some lovely men. Not many, but a few. This minister I mentioned?—he came one day this summer and sat with me on our porch . . . and we had ice cream and talked for over an hour. You know, when he left his previous church they gave him a Pontiac Grand Am. He made me realize something; he said that I seem to be in like a constant state of prayer. And it's true; every once in a while it stops me short, realizing it. It's like inside me I'm almost continually talking to the Lord. Not in words exactly . . . just—you know—communicating with Him. Or trying to. *Deeply excited, but suppressing it.* I tell you truthfully, if I can really come out of this I'm going to . . . I don't know what . . . fall in love with God. I think I have already.

KAREN: You're really beautiful.

PATRICIA: Oh no, dear, I'm a torn-off rag of my old self. The pills put ten years on my face. If he was a Jew or Italian or even Irish he'd be suing these doctors, but Yan-

kees never sue, you know. Although I have to say the
only thing he's been right about is medication.

KAREN: Your husband against pills?

PATRICIA: Fanatical. But of course he can stick his head out
the window and go high as a kite on a breath of fresh air.
Looks at her watch.

KAREN: I really think you're extremely attractive.

PATRICIA: No-no, dear, although I did win the county
beauty pageant when I was nineteen. But if you're talking
beauty you should have seen my mother. She only died
two years ago, age eighty-nine, but I still haven't gotten
over it. On the beach, right into her seventies, people
would still be staring at her—she had an unbelievable bust
right up to the end.

KAREN: I cut this finger once in a broken Coke machine.
But we never sued.

PATRICIA: Did your conversation always jump around? Because it could be your pills, believe me; the soul belongs
to God, we're not supposed to be stuffing Valium into
His mouth.

KAREN: I have a cousin who went right through the wind-
shield and she didn't get a cent. *Slight pause.* And it was
five below zero out. *Slight pause.* Her husband's Nor-
wegian.

PATRICIA: Look, dear, I know you're trying but don't feel you have to speak.

KAREN: No, I like speaking to you. Is he Baptist too, your husband?

PATRICIA: I said Methodist. But he's more Episcopal. But he'll go to any church if it's raining. *Slight pause.* I just don't know whether to tell him yet.

KAREN: What.

PATRICIA: That I'm off everything.

KAREN: But he'll like that, won't he?

PATRICIA: Oh yes. But he's going to be doubtful. —Which I am, too, let's face it—who can know for sure that you're going to stay clean? I don't want to fool myself, I've been on one medication or another for almost twenty years. But I do feel a thousand percent better. And I really have no idea how it happened. *Shakes her head.* Dear God, when I think of him hanging in there all these years . . . I'm so ashamed. But at the same time he's absolutely refused to make any money, every one of our children has had to work since they could practically write their names. I can't be expected to applaud, exactly. *Presses her eyes.* I guess sooner or later you just have to stand up and say, "I'm normal, I made it." But it's like standing on top of a stairs and there's no stairs. *Staring ahead.*

KAREN: I think I'd better go out to him. Should I tell your husband you're coming out?

PATRICIA: I think I'll wait a minute.

KAREN, *stands*. He seems very nice.

PATRICIA: —I'll tell you the truth, dear—I've put him through hell and I know it. . . . *Tears threaten her*. I know I have to stop blaming him; it came to me like a visitation two weeks ago, I-must-not-blame-Leroy-anymore. And it's amazing. I lost all desire for medication, I could feel it leaving me like a . . . like a ghost. *Slight pause*. It's just that he's got really well-to-do relatives and he simply will not accept anyone's help. I mean you take the Jews, the Italians, Irish—they've got their Italian-Americans, Irish-Americans, Hispanic-Americans—they stick together and help each other. But you ever hear of Yankee-Americans? Not on your life. Raise his taxes, rob him blind, the Yankee'll just sit there all alone getting sadder and sadder. —But I'm not going to think about it anymore.

KAREN: You have a very beautiful chin.

PATRICIA: Men with half his ability riding around in big expensive cars and now for the second Easter Sunday in a row his rear end collapsed.

KAREN: I think my license must have expired.

PATRICIA, *a surge of deep anger:* I refuse to ride around in a nine-year-old Chevrolet which was bought secondhand in the first place!

KAREN: They say there are only three keys for all General Motors cars. You suppose that's possible?

PATRICIA, *peremptorily now:* Believe me, dear, whatever they tell you, you have got to cut down the medication. It could be what's making your mind jump around . . .

KAREN: No, it's that you mentioned Chevrolet, which is General Motors, you see.

PATRICIA: Oh. . . . Well, let's just forget about it. *Slight pause.* Although you're probably right—here you're carefully locking your car and some crook is walking around with the same keys in his pocket. But everything's a fake, we all know that.

KAREN, *facing Patricia again:* I guess that would be depressing.

PATRICIA: No, that's not what depressed me . . .

KAREN: No, I meant him refusing to amount to anything and then spending money on banjo lessons.

PATRICIA: Did I tell you that?—I keep forgetting what I told you because I never know when you're listening. *Holds out her hand.* Here we go again. *Grasps her hand to stop the shaking.*

KAREN: —You sound like you had a wonderful courtship.

PATRICIA: Oh, Karen, everyone envied us, we were the handsomest pair in town; and I'm not boasting, believe me. *Breaks off; watches her hand shake and covers it again.* I just don't want to have to come back here again, you see. I don't think I could bear that. *Grips her hand, moving about.* I simply have to think positively. But it's unbelievable—he's seriously talking about donating his saw-and-chisel collection to the museum!—some of those tools are as old as the United States, they might be worth a fortune! —But I'm going to look ahead, that's all, just as straight ahead as a highway.

Slight pause.

KAREN: I feel so ashamed.

PATRICIA: For Heaven's sake, why? You've got a right to be depressed. There's more people in hospitals because of depression than any other disease.

KAREN: Is that true?

PATRICIA: Of course! Anybody with any sense has got to be depressed in this country. Unless you're really rich, I suppose. Don't let him shame you, dear.

KAREN: No . . . it's that you have so many thoughts.

PATRICIA: Oh. Well you can have thoughts, too—just remember your soul belongs to God and you mustn't be
shoving pills into His mouth.

Slight pause.

KAREN: We're rich, I think.

PATRICIA, *quickly interested:* . . . Really rich?

KAREN: He's got the oil delivery now, and of course he
always had the fertilizer and the Chevy dealership, and of
course the lumber yard and all. And Isuzus now.

PATRICIA: What's Isuzus?

KAREN: It's a Japanese car.

PATRICIA: . . . I'll just never catch up.

KAREN: We go to Arkansas in the spring.

PATRICIA: Arkansas?

KAREN: For the catfish. It's where I broke down. But I can't
help it, the sight of catfish makes me want to vomit. Not
that I was trying to . . . you know . . . do anything. I just
read the instructions on the bottle wrong. Do you mind
if I ask you something?

PATRICIA: I hope it's nothing personal, is it?

KAREN: Well I don't know.

PATRICIA: . . . Well go ahead, what is it?

KAREN: Do you shop in the A&P or Stop & Shop?

PATRICIA: . . . I'm wondering if you've got the wrong medication. But I guess you'll never overdose—you vomit at the drop of a hat. It may be your secret blessing.

KAREN: —He wants to get me out of the house more, but it's hard to make up my mind where.

PATRICIA: Well . . . A&P is good. Or Stop & Shop. More or less. Kroger's is good for fish sometimes.

KAREN: Which do you like best? I'll go where you go.

PATRICIA: You're very flattering. *Stands, inner excitement.* It's amazing—I'm really beginning to feel wonderful; maybe I ought to go home with him today. I mean what does it come down to, really?—it's simply a question of confidence . . .

KAREN: I wish we could raise some vegetables like we did on the farm. Do you?

PATRICIA: Oh, he raises things in our yard. Healthy things like salsify and collards—and kale. You ever eat kale?

KAREN: I can't remember kale.

PATRICIA: You might as well salt your shower curtain and chop it up with a tomato.

KAREN: —So . . . meats are . . . which?—A&P?

PATRICIA: No. Meats are Stop & Shop. I'm really thinking I might go home today. It's just not his fault, I have to remember that . . .

KAREN: But staples?

PATRICIA: What? —Oh. Stop & Shop.

KAREN: Then what's for A&P?

PATRICIA: Vegetables.

KAREN: Oh right. And Kroger's?

PATRICIA: Why don't you just forget Kroger's.

KAREN, *holds up five fingers, bends one at a time.* . . . Then Stop & Shop . . .

PATRICIA: Maybe it's that you're trying to remember three things. Whyn't you just do A&P and Stop & Shop.

Slight pause.

KAREN: I kind of liked Kroger's.

PATRICIA: Then go to Kroger's, for Heaven's sake!

KAREN: Well I guess I'll go out to him. *Moves to go. Halts.* I hope you aren't really leaving today, are you?

PATRICIA, *higher tension:* I'm deciding.

KAREN: Well . . . here I go, I guess. *Halts again.* I meant to tell you, I kind of like the banjo. It's very good with tap dancing.

PATRICIA: Tap dancing.

KAREN: There's a tap teacher lives on our road.

PATRICIA: You tap-dance?

KAREN: Well John rented a video of Ginger Rogers and Fred Astaire, and I kind of liked it. I can sing "Cheek to Cheek"? Would you like to hear it?

PATRICIA: Sure, go ahead—this is certainly a surprise.

KAREN, *sings in a frail voice:* "Heaven, I'm in heaven, and the cares that clung around me through the week . . ."

PATRICIA: That's beautiful, Karen! Listen, what exactly does Doctor Rockwell say about you?

KAREN: Well, he says it's quite common when a woman is home alone all day.

PATRICIA: What's common?

KAREN: Something moving around in the next room?

PATRICIA: Oh, I see. —You have any idea who it is?

KAREN: My mother. —My husband might bring my tap shoes and tails . . . but he probably forgot. I have a high hat and shorts too. And a walking stick? But would they allow dancing in here?

PATRICIA: They might. But of course the minute they see you enjoying yourself they'll probably try to knock you out with a pill.

Karen makes to go, halts again.

KAREN: Did your mother like you?

PATRICIA: Oh yes. We were all very close. Didn't yours?

KAREN: No. She left the whole farm to her cousin. Tell about your family, can you? Were they really all blond?

PATRICIA: Oh as blond as the tassels on Golden Bantam corn . . . everybody'd turn and look when we went by. My mother was perfection. We all were, I guess. *With a chuckle.* You know, we had a flat roof extending from the house over the garage, and mother and my sisters and me—on the first warm spring days we used to sunbathe out there.

KAREN, *covering her mouth:* No! You mean nude?

PATRICIA: Nudity doesn't matter that much in Sweden, and we were all brought up to love the sun. And we'd near die laughing because the minute we dropped our robes— you know how quiet a town Grenville is—you could hear the footsteps going up the clock tower over the Presbyterian church, and we pretended not to notice but that little narrow tower was just packed with Presbyterians.

KAREN: Good lord!

PATRICIA: We'd stretch out and pretend not to see a thing. And then my mother'd sit up suddenly and point up at the steeple and yell, "Boo!" And they'd all go running down the stairs like mice!

They both enjoy the laugh.

KAREN: I think your husband's very good-looking, isn't he.

PATRICIA: He is, but my brothers . . . I mean the way they stood, and walked . . . and their teeth! Charles won the All–New England golf tournament, and Buzz came within a tenth of an inch of the gold medal in the pole vault— that was in the Portugal Olympics.

KAREN: My! Do you still get together much?

PATRICIA: Oh, they're all gone now.

KAREN: Moved away?

PATRICIA: No . . . dead.

KAREN: Oh my. They overstrain?

PATRICIA: Buzz hung himself on his wife's closet door.

KAREN: Oh my!

PATRICIA: Eight days later Charles shot himself on the tractor.

KAREN, *softly:* Oh my. Did they leave a note or anything?

PATRICIA: No. But we all knew what it was.

KAREN: Can you say?

PATRICIA: Disappointment. We were all brought up expecting to be wonderful, and . . . *breaks off with a shrug* . . . just wasn't.

KAREN: Well . . . here I go.

> *Karen exits. Patricia stares ahead for a moment in a blankly reminiscent mood. Now she looks at her face in a mirror, smoothing wrinkles away . . .*

> *Leroy enters.*

PATRICIA: I was just coming out.

LEROY: 'Cause Mrs. Frick . . .

PATRICIA, *cuts him off by drawing his head down and stroking his cheek. And in a soft but faintly patronizing tone* . . . I was just coming out, Leroy. You don't have to repeat everything. Come, sit with me and let's not argue.

LEROY: . . . How's your day been?

> *She is still moved by her brothers' memory; also, she hasn't received something she hoped for from him. She shrugs and turns her head away.*

PATRICIA: I've had worse.

LEROY: Did you wash your hair?

PATRICIA, *pleased he noticed:* How can you tell?

LEROY: Looks livelier. Is that nail polish?

PATRICIA: M-hm.

LEROY: Good. You're looking good, Patty.

PATRICIA: I'm feeling better. Not completely but a lot.

LEROY, *nods approvingly.* Great! Did he change your medication or something?

PATRICIA: No.

LEROY: Something different about you.

PATRICIA, *mysteriously excited:* You think so?

LEROY: Your eyes are clearer. You seem more like you're
. . . connecting.

PATRICIA: I am, I think. But I warn you, I'm nervous.

LEROY: That's okay. Your color is more . . . I don't know
. . . vigorous.

PATRICIA: Is it? *She touches her face.*

LEROY: You look almost like years ago . . .

PATRICIA: Something's happened but I don't want to talk
about it yet.

LEROY: Really? Like what?

PATRICIA, *instant resistance:* I just said I . . .

LEROY: . . . Okay. *Goes to a window.* —It looks like rain
outside, but we can walk around if you like. They've got
a beautiful tulip bed down there; the colors really shine
in this gray light. Reds and purple and whites, and a gray.
Never saw a tulip be that kind of gray.

PATRICIA: How's Amelia's leg? Are you getting her to change her bandage?

LEROY: Yes. But she'd better stop thinking she can drive a car.

PATRICIA: Well, why don't you tell her?

LEROY, *a little laugh.* That'll be the day, won't it, when she starts listening to her father.

PATRICIA, *a softness despite her language:* She might if you laid down the law without just complaining. And if she could hear something besides disappointment in your voice.

LEROY: She's learned to look down at me, Patty, you know that.

PATRICIA, *strongly, but nearly a threat of weeping.* Well, I hope you're not blaming me for that.

LEROY, *he holds back, stands silent. Then puffs out his cheeks and blows, shaking his head with a defensive grin.* Not my day, I see.

PATRICIA: Maybe it could have been.

LEROY: I was looking forward to telling you something.

PATRICIA: What.

LEROY: I got Harrelson to agree to twelve-thousand-five for the altar.

PATRICIA: There, you see!—and you were so glad to accept eight. I told you . . . !

LEROY: I give you all the credit. I finally got it through my thick skull, I said to myself, okay, you are slower than most, but quality's got a right to be slow. And he didn't make a peep—twelve thousand, five hundred dollars.

She looks at him, immensely sad.

—Well why do you look so sad?

PATRICIA: Come here. *Draws him down, kisses him.* I'm glad. . . . I just couldn't help thinking of all these years wasted trying to get you to charge enough; but I've decided to keep looking straight ahead, not back—I'm very glad you got the twelve. You've done a wonderful thing.

LEROY, *excited:* Listen, what has he got you on?

PATRICIA: Well, I'm still a long way from perfect, but I . . .

LEROY: Patty, nothing's perfect except a hot bath.

PATRICIA: It's nothing to joke about. I told you I'm nervous, I'm not used to . . . to . . .

LEROY: He changed your medication, didn't he.

PATRICIA: I just don't want you to think I have no problems anymore.

LEROY: Oh, I'd never think that, Patty. Has he put you on something new?

PATRICIA: *He* hasn't done anything.

Pause.

LEROY: Okay, I'll shut up.

> *She sweeps her hair back; he silently observes her. Then . . .*

. . . This Mr. Frick handles oil burners; I don't know if I can trust him but he says he'd give me a good buy. We could use a new burner.

PATRICIA: What would you say if I said I'm thinking of coming home.

LEROY, *a pause filled with doubt.* You are? When?

PATRICIA: Maybe next Thursday. For good.

LEROY: Uh huh.

PATRICIA: You don't sound very positive.

LEROY: You know you're the only one can make that decision, Pat. You want to come home I'm always happy to take you home.

Slight pause.

PATRICIA: I feel if I could look ahead just the right amount I'd be all right.

LEROY: What do you mean?

PATRICIA: I realized something lately; when I'm home I have a tendency—especially in the afternoons when everybody's out and I'm alone—I look very far ahead. What I should do is only look ahead a little bit, like to the evening or the next day. And then it's all right. It's when I start looking years ahead . . . *slight pause* . . . You once told me why you think I got sick. I've forgotten . . . what did you say?

LEROY: What do I really know about it, Pat?

PATRICIA: Why do you keep putting yourself down?—you've got to stop imitating your father. There are things you know very well. —Remind me what you said . . . Why am I sick?

LEROY: I always thought it was your family

PATRICIA, *fingers pressing on her eyes:* I want to concentrate. Go on.

LEROY: They were so close, they were all over each other, and you all had this—you know—very high opinion of yourselves; each and every one of you was automatically going to go to the head of the line just because your name was Sorgenson. And life isn't that way, so you got sick.

Long pause; she stares, nodding.

PATRICIA: You've had no life at all, have you.

LEROY: I wouldn't say that.

PATRICIA: I can't understand how I never saw it.

LEROY: Why?—it's been great watching the kids growing up; and I've had some jobs I've enjoyed . . .

PATRICIA: But not your wife.

LEROY: It's a long time since I blamed you, Pat. It's your upbringing.

LEROY: Well I could blame yours too, couldn't I.

LEROY: You sure could.

PATRICIA: I mean this constant optimism is very irritating when you're fifty times more depressed than I am.

LEROY: Now Patty, you know that's not . . .

PATRICIA: You are depressed, Leroy! Because you're scared of people, you really don't trust anyone, and that's incidentally why you never made any money. You could have set the world on fire but you can't bear to work along with other human beings.

LEROY: The last human being I took on to help me tried to steal my half-inch Stanley chisel.

PATRICIA: You mean you *think* he tried . . .

LEROY: I didn't think anything, I found it in his tool box. And that's an original Stanley, not the junk they sell today.

PATRICIA: So what!

LEROY: So what?—that man has three grandchildren! And he's a Chapman—that's one of the oldest upstanding families in the county.

PATRICIA, *emphatically, her point proved:* Which is why you're depressed.

LEROY, *laughs.* I'm not, but why shouldn't I be?—a Chapman stealing a chisel? I mean God Almighty, they've had generals in that family, secretaries of state or some goddam thing. Anyway, if I'm depressed it's from something that happened, not something I imagine.

PATRICIA: I feel like a log that keeps bumping against another log in the middle of the river.

LEROY: Boy, you're a real roller coaster. We were doing great there for a minute, what got us off on this?

PATRICIA: I can't be at peace when I know you are full of denial, and that's saying it straight.

LEROY: What denial? *Laughs.* You want me to say I'm a failure?

PATRICIA: That is not what I . . .

LEROY: Hey, I know what—I'll get a bumper sticker printed up—"The driver of this car is a failure!" —I betcha I could sell a hundred million of them . . . *A sudden fury:* . . . Or maybe I should just drive out on a tractor and shoot myself!

PATRICIA: That's a terrible thing to say to me, Leroy!

LEROY: Well I'm sorry, Patty, but I'm not as dumb as I look—I'm never going to win if I have to compete against your brothers!

PATRICIA, *chastened for the moment:* I did not say you're a failure.

LEROY: I didn't mean to yell; I'm sorry. I know you don't mean to sound like you do, sometimes.

PATRICIA, *unable to retrieve:* I said nothing about a failure. *On the verge of weeping.*

LEROY: It's okay, maybe I am a failure; but in my opinion no more than the rest of this country.

PATRICIA: What happened?—I thought this visit started off so nicely.

LEROY: Maybe you're not used to being so alert; you've been so lethargic for a long time, you know.

She moves; he watches her.

I'm sure of it, Pat, if you could only find two ounces of trust I know we could still have a life.

PATRICIA: I know. *Slight pause; she fights down tears.* What did you have in mind, exactly, when you said it was my upbringing?

LEROY: I don't know . . . I had a flash of your father, that time long ago when we were sitting on your porch . . . we were getting things ready for our wedding . . . and right in front of you he turns to me cool as a cucumber and says—*through laughter, mimicking Swedish accent*—"No Yankee will ever be good enough for a Swedish girl." I nearly fell off into the rosebushes.

PATRICIA, *laughs with a certain delight.* Well, he was old-fashioned . . .

LEROY, *laughing:* Yeah, a real old-fashioned welcome into the family!

PATRICIA: Well, the Yankees *were* terrible to us.

LEROY: That's a hundred years ago, Pat.

PATRICIA, *starting to anger:* You shouldn't keep denying this!
——They paid them fifty cents a week and called us dumb
Swedes with strong backs and weak minds and did noth-
ing but make us ridiculous.

LEROY: But, Patty, if you walk around town today there
isn't a good piece of property that isn't owned by Swedes.

PATRICIA: But that's now.

LEROY: Well when are we living?

PATRICIA: We were treated like animals, some Yankee doctors wouldn't come out to a Swedish home to deliver a
baby . . .

LEROY, *laughs.* Well all I hope is that I'm the last Yankee
so people can start living today instead of a hundred years
ago.

PATRICIA: There was something else you said. About standing on line.

LEROY: On line?

PATRICIA: That you'll always be at the head of the line because . . . *breaks off.*

LEROY: I'm the only one on it.

PATRICIA: . . . Is that really true? You do compete, don't you? You must, at least in your mind?

LEROY: Only with myself. We're really all on a one-person line, Pat. I learned that in these years.

Pause. She stares ahead.

PATRICIA: That's very beautiful. Where'd you get that idea?

LEROY: I guess I made it up, I don't know. It's up to you, Pat—if you feel you're ready, let's go home. Now or Thursday or whenever. What about medication?

PATRICIA, *makes herself ready.* I wasn't going to tell you for another week or two, till I'm absolutely rock sure; —I've stopped taking anything for . . . this is twenty-one days.

LEROY: *Anything?*

She nods with a certain suspense.

My God, Patty. And you feel all right?

PATRICIA: . . . I haven't felt this way in—fifteen years. I've no idea why, but I forgot to take anything, and I slept right through till morning, and I woke up and it was like . . . I'd been blessed during the night. And I haven't had anything since.

LEROY: Did I tell you or didn't I!

PATRICIA: But it's different for you. You're not addictive . . .

LEROY: But didn't I tell you all that stuff is poison? I'm just flying, Patty.

PATRICIA, *clasps her hands to steady herself:* But I'm afraid about coming home. I don't know if I'm jumping the gun. I *feel* I could, but . . .

LEROY: Well, let's talk about it. Is it a question of trusting yourself? Because I think if you've come this far . . .

PATRICIA: Be quiet a minute! *She holds his hand.* Why have you stayed with me?

LEROY, *laughs.* God knows!

PATRICIA: I've been very bad to you sometimes, Leroy, I really see that now. *Starting to weep.* Tell me the truth; in all these years, have you gone to other women? I wouldn't blame you, I just want to know.

LEROY: Well I've thought of it but I never did anything.

PATRICIA, *looking deeply into his eyes:* You really haven't, have you.

LEROY: No.

PATRICIA: Why?

LEROY: I just kept hoping you'd come out of this.

PATRICIA: But it's been so long.

LEROY: I know.

PATRICIA: Even when I'd . . . throw things at you?

LEROY: Uh uh.

PATRICIA: Like that time with the roast?

LEROY: Well, that's one time I came pretty close. But I knew it was those damned pills, not you.

PATRICIA: But why would you be gone night after night? That was a woman, wasn't it.

LEROY: No. Some nights I went over to the library basement to practice banjo with Phil Palumbo. Or to Manny's Diner for some donuts and talk to the fellas.

PATRICIA, *slightest tinge of suspicion:* There are fellas there at *night*?

LEROY: Sure; working guys, mostly young single fellas. But some with wives. You know—have a beer, watch TV.

PATRICIA: And women?

LEROY, *a short beat.* —You know, Pat—and I'm not criticizing—but wouldn't it better for you to try believing a person instead of trying not to believe?

PATRICIA: I'm just wondering if you know . . . there's lots of women would love having you. But you probably don't know that, do you.

LEROY: Sure I do.

PATRICIA: You know lots of women would love to have you?

LEROY: . . . Well, yes, I know that.

PATRICIA: Really. How do you know that?

LEROY, *his quick, open laugh:* I can tell.

PATRICIA: Then what's keeping you? Why don't you move out?

LEROY: Pat, you're torturing me.

PATRICIA: I'm trying to find myself!

> *She moves in stress, warding off an explosion. There is angry resentment in his voice.*

LEROY: I'd remember you happy and loving—that's what kept me; as long ago as that is now, I'd remember how you'd pull on your stockings and get a little makeup on and pin up your hair. . . . When you're positive about life there's just nobody like you. Nobody. Not in life, not in the movies, not on TV. *Slight pause.* But I'm not going to deny it—if it wasn't for the kids I probably *would* have gone.

She is silent, but loaded with something unspoken.

You're wanting to tell me something, aren't you.

PATRICIA: . . . I know what a lucky woman I've been.

LEROY, *he observes her.* —What is it, you want me to stop coming to see you for a while? Please tell me, Pat; there's something on your mind.

Pause. She forces it out.

PATRICIA: I know I shouldn't feel this way, but I'm not too sure I could stand it, knowing that it's never going to . . . I mean, will it ever change anymore?

LEROY: You mean—is it ever going to be "wonderful."

She looks at him, estimating.

Well—no, I guess this is pretty much it; although to me it's already wonderful—I mean the kids, and there are some clear New England mornings when you want to drink the air and the sunshine.

PATRICIA: You can make more out of a change in temperature than any human being I ever heard of—I can't live on weather!

LEROY: Pat, we're getting old! This is just about as rich and handsome as I'm ever going to be and as good as you're ever going to look, so you want to be with me or not?

PATRICIA: I don't want to fool either of us . . . I can't bear it when you can't pay the bills . . .

LEROY: But I'm a carpenter—this is probably the way it's been for carpenters since they built Noah's ark. What do you want to do?

PATRICIA: I'm honestly not sure I could hold up. Not when I hear your sadness all the time and your eyes are full of disappointment. You seem . . . *breaks off.*

LEROY: . . . How do I seem?

PATRICIA: I shouldn't say it.

LEROY: . . . Beaten. Like it's all gone by. *Hurt, but holding on:* All right, Patty, then I might as well say it—I don't think you *ever* had a medical problem; you have an attitude problem . . .

PATRICIA: My problem is spiritual.

LEROY: Okay, I don't mind callling it spiritual.

PATRICIA: Well that's a new note; I thought these ministers were all quacks.

LEROY: Not all; but the ones who make house calls with women, eating up all the ice cream, are not my idea of spiritual.

PATRICIA: *You* know what spiritual is?

LEROY: For me? Sure. Ice skating.

PATRICIA: Ice skating is spiritual.

LEROY: Yes, and skiing! To me spiritual is whatever makes me forget myself and feel happy to be alive. Like even a well-sharpened saw, or a perfect compound joint.

PATRICIA: Maybe this is why we can't get along—spiritual is nothing you can see, Leroy.

LEROY: Really! Then why didn't God make everything invisible! We are in this world and you're going to have to find some way to love it!

Her eyes are filling with tears.

Pounding on me is not going to change anything to wonderful, Patty.

She seems to be receiving him.

I'll say it again, because it's the only thing that's kept me
from going crazy—you just have to love this world. *He
comes to her, takes her hand.* Come home. Maybe it'll take
a while, but I really believe you can make it.

Uncertainty filling her face . . .

All right, don't decide now, I'll come back Thursday and
we'll see then.

PATRICIA: Where you going now?

LEROY: For my banjo lesson. I'm learning a new number.
—I'll play it for you if you want to hear it.

PATRICIA, *hesitates, then kisses him.* Couldn't you do it on
guitar?

LEROY: It's not the same on guitar. *He goes to his banjo case
and opens it.*

PATRICIA: But banjo sounds so picky.

LEROY: But that's what's good about it, it's clean, like a
toothpick . . .

Enter the Fricks.

LEROY: Oh hi, Mrs. Frick.

KAREN: He brought my costume. Would you care to see it? *To Frick:* This is her—Mrs. Hamilton.

FRICK: Oh! How do you do?

KAREN: This is my husband.

PATRICIA: How do you do?

FRICK: She's been telling me all about you. *Shaking Patricia's hand:* I want to say that I'm thankful to you.

PATRICIA: Really? What for?

FRICK: Well what she says you've been telling her. About her attitude and all.

KAREN, *to Patricia:* Would you like to see my costume? I also have a blue one, but . . .

FRICK, *overriding her:* . . . By the way, I'm Frick Lumber, I recognized your husband right away . . .

KAREN: Should I put it on?

PATRICIA: Sure, put it on!

Leroy starts tuning his banjo.

FRICK, *to Patricia:* All it is is a high hat and shorts, y'know . . . nothing much to it.

KAREN, *to Frick:* Shouldn't I?

PATRICIA: Why not, for Heaven's sake?

FRICK: Go ahead, if they want to see it. *Laughs to Patricia.* She found it in a catalogue. I think it's kinda silly at her age, but I admit I'm a conservative kind of person . . .

KAREN, *cutting him off, deeply embarrassed:* I'll only be a minute. *She starts out, and stops, and to Patricia:* You really think I should?

PATRICIA: Of course!

FRICK, *suppressing an angry embarrassment:* Karen, honey, if you're going to do it, do it.

    Karen exits with valise. Leroy tunes his instrument.

FRICK: The slightest decision, she's got to worry it into the ground. —But I have to tell you, it's years since I've seen this much life in her, she's like day and night. What exactly'd you say to her? *To Leroy, thumbing toward Patricia:* She says she just opened up her eyes . . .

LEROY, *surprised:* Patricia?

FRICK: I have to admit, it took me a while to realize it's a sickness . . .

PATRICIA: You're not the only one.

FRICK: Looked to me like she was just favoring herself; I mean the woman has everything, what right has she got to start shooting blanks like that? I happen to be a great believer in self-discipline, started from way down below sea level myself, sixty acres of rocks and swampland is all we had. That's why I'm so glad that somebody's talked to her with your attitude.

PATRICIA, *vamping for time:* What . . . what attitude do you mean?

FRICK: Just that you're so . . . so positive.

Leroy looks up at Patricia, thunderstruck.

She says you made her realize all the things she could be doing instead of mooning around all day . . .

PATRICIA: Well I think being positive is the only way.

FRICK: That's just what I tell her . . .

PATRICIA: But you have to be careful not to sound so disappointed in her.

FRICK: I sound disappointed?

PATRICIA: In a way, I think. —She's got to feel treasured, you see.

FRICK: I appreciate that, but the woman can stand in one place for half an hour at a time practically without moving.

PATRICIA: Well that's the sickness, you see.

FRICK: I realize that. But she won't even go shopping . . .

PATRICIA: You see? You're sounding disappointed in her.

FRICK, *angering:* I am not disappointed in her! I'm just telling you the situation!

PATRICIA: Mr. Frick, she's standing under a mountain a mile high—you've got to help her over it. That woman has very big possibilities!

FRICK: Think so.

PATRICIA: Absolutely.

FRICK: I hope you're right. *To Leroy, indicating Patricia:* You don't mind my saying it, you could do with a little of her optimism.

LEROY, *turns from Patricia, astonished.* Huh?

FRICK, *to Patricia, warmly:* Y'know, she made me have a little platform built down the cellar, with a big full-length mirror so she could see herself dance . . .

PATRICIA: But do you spend time watching her . . .

FRICK: Well she says not to till she's good at it.

PATRICIA: That's because she's terrified of your criticism.

FRICK: But I haven't made any criticism.

PATRICIA: But do you like tap dancing?

FRICK: Well I don't know, I never thought about it one way or another.

PATRICIA: Well that's the thing, you see. It happens to mean a great deal to her . . .

FRICK: I'm for it, I don't mean I'm not for it. But don't tell me you think it's normal for a woman her age to be getting out of bed two, three in the morning and start practicing.

PATRICIA: Well maybe she's trying to get you interested in it. Are you?

FRICK: In tap dancing? Truthfully, no.

PATRICIA: Well there you go . . .

FRICK: Well we've got a lot of new competition in our fuel-oil business . . .

PATRICIA: Fuel oil!

FRICK: I've got seven trucks on the road that I've got to keep busy . . .

PATRICIA: Well there you go, maybe that's why your wife is in here.

FRICK, *visibly angering:* Well I can't be waked up at two o'clock in the morning and be any good next day, now can I. She's not normal.

PATRICIA: Normal! They've got whole universities debating what's normal. Who knows what's normal, Mr. Frick?

FRICK: You mean getting out of bed at two o'clock in the morning and putting on a pair of tap shoes is a common occurrence in this country? I don't think so. —But I didn't mean to argue when you're . . . not feeling well.

PATRICIA: I've never felt better.

She turns away, and Frick looks with bewildered surprise to Leroy, who returns him a look of suppressed laughter.

FRICK: Well you sure know how to turn somebody inside out.

Karen enters; she is dressed in satin shorts, a tailcoat, a high hat, tap shoes, and as they turn to look at her, she pulls out a collapsible walking stick, and strikes a theatrical pose.

PATRICIA: Well now, don't you look great!

KAREN, *desperate for reassurance:* You really like it?

LEROY: That looks terrific!

PATRICIA: Do a step!

KAREN: I don't have my tape. *Turns to Frick, timorously:* But if you'd sing "Swanee River . . ."

FRICK: Oh Karen, for God's sake!

PATRICIA: I can sing it . . .

KAREN: He knows my speed. Please, John . . . just for a minute.

FRICK: All right, go ahead. *Unhappily, he sings:* "Way down upon the Swanee River . . ."

KAREN: Wait, you're too fast . . .

FRICK, *slower and angering:* "Way—down—upon—the—Swanee River,
Far, far away.
That's where my heart is turning ever . . ."
[*etc.*]

Karen taps out her number, laboriously but for a short stretch with a promise of grace. Frick continues singing . . .

PATRICIA: Isn't she wonderful?

LEROY: Hey, she's great!

Karen dances a bit more boldly, a joyous freedom starting into her.

PATRICIA: She's marvelous! Look at her, Mr. Frick!

A hint of the sensuous in Karen now; Frick, embarrassed, uneasily avoids more than a glance at his wife.

FRICK: ". . . everywhere I roam . . ."

PATRICIA: Will you look at her!

FRICK, *hard-pressed, explodes: I am looking at her, goddammit!*

This astonishing furious shout, his reddened face, stops everything. A look of fear is on Karen's face.

KAREN, *apologetically to Patricia:* He *was* looking at me . . . *To Frick:* She didn't mean you *weren't* looking, she meant . . .

FRICK, *rigidly repressing his anger and embarrassment:* I've got to run along now.

KAREN: I'm so sorry, John, but she . . .

FRICK, *rigidly:* Nothing to be sorry about, dear. Very nice to have met you folks.

He starts to exit. Karen moves to intercept him.

KAREN: Oh John, I hope you're not . . . [going to be angry.]

JOHN: I'm just fine. *He sees her despair coming on.* What are you looking so sad about?—you danced great . . .

She is immobile.

I'm sorry to've raised my voice but it don't mean I'm disappointed, dear. You understand? *A nervous glance toward Patricia. Stiffly, with enormous effort:* . . . You . . . you danced better than I ever saw you.

She doesn't change.

Now look here, Karen, I hope you don't feel I'm . . . disappointed or something, you hear . . . ? 'Cause I'm not. And that's definite.

She keeps staring at him.

I'll try to make it again on Friday. —Keep it up.

He abruptly turns and exits.

Karen stands perfectly still, staring at nothing.

PATRICIA: Karen?

> *Karen seems not to hear, standing there facing the empty door in her high hat and costume.*

How about Leroy playing it for you? *To Leroy:* Play it.

LEROY: I could on the guitar, but I never did on this . . .

PATRICIA: Well couldn't you try it?—I don't know what good that thing is.

LEROY: Well here . . . let me see.

> *He picks out "Swanee River" on his banjo, but Karen doesn't move.*

PATRICIA: There you go, Karen! Try it, I love your dancing! Come on . . . *Sings:* "Way down upon the Swanee river . . ."

> *Karen now breaks her motionlessly depressed mode and looks at Patricia. Leroy continues playing, humming along with it. His picking is getting more accurate . . .*

PATRICIA: Is it the right tempo? Tell him!

KAREN, *very very softly:* Could you play a little faster?

> *Leroy speeds it up. With an unrelieved sadness, Karen goes into her number, does a few steps, but stops. Leroy gradually stops playing. Karen walks out. Patricia starts to follow her but gives it up and comes to a halt.*
>
> *Leroy turns to Patricia, who is staring ahead. Now she turns to Leroy.*
>
> *He meets her gaze, his face filled with inquiry. He comes to her and stands there.*
>
> *For a long moment neither of them moves. Then she reaches out and touches his face—there is a muted gratitude in her gesture.*
>
> *She goes to a closet and takes a small overnight bag to the bed and puts her things into it.*
>
> *Leroy watches her for a moment, then stows his banjo in its case, and stands waiting for her. She starts to put on a light coat. He comes and helps her into it.*
>
> *Her face is charged with her struggle against her self-doubt.*

LEROY, *laughs, but about to weep:* Ready?

PATRICIA, *filling up:* Leroy . . .

LEROY: One day at a time, Pat—you're already twenty-one ahead. Kids are going to be so happy to have you home.

PATRICIA: I can't believe it. . . . I've had nothing.

LEROY: It's a miracle.

PATRICIA: Thank you. *Breaking through her own resistance, she draws him to her and kisses him. Grinning tauntingly:* . . . That car going to get us home?

LEROY, *laughs:* Stop picking on that car, it's all checked out!

>   *They start toward the door, he carrying her bag and his banjo.*

PATRICIA: Once you believe in something you just never know when to stop, do you.

LEROY: Well there's very little rust, and the new ones aren't half as well built . . .

PATRICIA: Waste not, want not.

LEROY: Well I really don't *go* for those new Chevies . . .

>   *She walks out, he behind her. Their voices are heard . . .*

PATRICIA: Between the banjo and that car I've certainly got a whole lot to look forward to.

>   *His laughter sounds down the corridor.*

The woman on the bed stirs, then falls back and remains motionless. A stillness envelops the whole stage.

END.

I

When I began writing plays in the late thirties, something called realism was the undisputed reigning style in the American commercial theatre—which was just about all the theatre there was in this country. The same was more or less the case in Britain. If not a mass art, theatre then could still be thought of at least as a popular one, although everyone knew—long before television—that something of its common appeal had gone out of it, and a lot of its twenties' glamour, too. One blamed the movies, which had stolen so much of the audience and thus theatre's old dominance as a cultural influence. Notwithstanding the obvious fact that the audience was predominantly middle class, we continued to imagine that we were making plays for people of many different educational and cultural levels, a representative variety of the city and even the country. If this was never really true, there was certainly no thought of appealing to a clique of college graduates or to academics and their standards. A *New York Times* critic like George S. Kaufman had both feet in show business and became the most popular writer of comedies of the period, while Brooks Atkinson may have had one eye on Aristotle but understood that his readers were Americans impatient with any theatrical enterprise that required either education or patience. Outside New York there were at least the remains of the twenties' touring wheel, theatres in many smaller cities regularly attended by quite ordinary citizens eager for last year's Broadway hits, albeit with replacement casts. In New York, with a ticket price of fifty-five cents to four dollars and forty cents, one somehow took for granted that a professor might be sitting next to a housewife, a priest beside a skilled worker or perhaps a grammar-school teacher, a small or large business executive beside a student. This conception of the demotic audience, accurate or not, influenced the writing of plays directed at the commonsensical experience of everyday people. Missing were black or Asian or Hispanic faces, of course, but they were beyond the consciousness of the prevailing culture. As for production costs, even into the forties they were within reason; plays like *All My Sons* or *Death of a Salesman*, for example, cost between twenty and forty thousand to produce, a budget small enough to be raised by half a dozen modest contributors, who might lose all, with some embarrassment but reasonably little pain, or make a killing.

Radicals—people like myself, trying to convince ourselves that we were carrying on the age-old tradition of theatre as a civic art rather than a purely commercial one— were in a conflict; to attract even the fitful interest of a Broadway producer, and subsequently to engage the audience, we had to bow to realism, even if the poetic forms were what we really admired or at least wished to explore. An Expressionist like the German Ernst Toller, for example, would not have been read past his sixth page by a Broadway producer or, for that matter, one in London. Among the playwrights one thinks of as important, not one was—or is now—welcome in the commercial theatre. Not Chekhov, not Ibsen, not Hauptmann, not Pirandello, Strindberg, Turgenev—not even Shaw. To so much as think of performing a Beckett play like *Waiting for Godot* in the general proximity of Broadway a cast of movie stars and a short run are essential—Lincoln Center pulled it off in 1988—and things were probably a bit worse half a century ago. One need only read O'Neill's letters of complaint at the "showshop" of Broadway and the narrow compass of the American audience's imagination—or in Britain, Shaw's ridicule of his countrymen's provincialism—to understand the problem; for some mysterious reason the Anglo-Saxon culture regarded theatre as an entertainment first and last, an art of escape with none of the Continental or Russian interest in moral and philosophical opportunities or obligations. Very occasionally in America there was an *Adding Machine* by the young Elmer Rice, but such a breakout from conventional realism was rare enough to be brought up in conversation for years after, like a calf born with five legs. The English-language theatre was pridefully commercial, a profit-making enterprise which wed it to a form whose surfaces of familiar reality would be universally recognized. Captain Shotover's outcry, "I like to know where I am!" could have been sewn to the flag of this theatre. Only musicals had the happy license to stretch reality, at least to some extent. But for straight plays, even satire was too strange to prosper; George Kaufman defined satire as what closes on Saturday night.

The point here is that what we think of as "straight realism" was tiresome half a century ago, indeed longer ago than that, but it was accepted by the audiences and almost all the reviewers as a reflection of life. Nonetheless it should be remembered that realism has reemerged at various moments to very capably express the essence of an era. At a time when "experimental" is all the virtue a play needs in order to gain serious consideration, it is not a bad idea to confess that an extraordinarily few such researches have achieved any kind of enduring life. It is not quite enough to know how to escape; one has also to think of arriving somewhere.

In the thirties, probably the single exception—at least that I was aware of—to realism's domination was the WPA's *Living Newspaper*, the one formal innovation of American theatre. An epic in more or less presentational form, written like movies by groups of writers, rather than individually, it dealt in an overtly exuberant spirit with social issues like public ownership of electrical power, labor unions, agriculture, and medicine, and was extremely popular. Significantly, the WPA was government-subsidized, and did not have to make a profit. Using unemployed actors, designers, technicians, a show could call upon large casts and elaborate scenery and production elements. And the ticket was low-priced. The WPA could send Orson Welles, for example, into Harlem storefronts with a big cast playing *Doctor Faustus*, charging a quarter a seat. But theatre-for-profit was hardly affected by what might be called this epic-populist approach—it was simply too expensive to produce.

I mention these mundane matters because they profoundly affect style in the theatre, which, like politics, is always the art of the possible.

There were at least a dozen playwrights regularly feeding the commercial theatre in the years before World War II, and all but perhaps Odets and Hellman would have pridefully declared that their sole purpose was to entertain. Those playwrights were sophisticated and no doubt knew all about the Continental theatre tradition, and its aspiring to the philosophical condition, something like that of the Greeks or, in a different way, the Elizabethans. The Theatre Guild, for one, had been started in the twenties in part to bring that kind of theatre to America, the theatre of Pirandello, Schnitzler, Ibsen, and Strindberg.

In the thirties, one American styled himself a political revolutionary, and that was Clifford Odets. O'Neill, of course, had been the aesthetic rebel but his socialism was private rather than informing his plays, although *The Hairy Ape* is surely an anticapitalist work. It was his formal experiments and tragic mood that set him apart. O'Neill was a totally isolated phenomenon in the Broadway theatre as a maker and user of new and old theatrical forms.

Odets, on the other hand, while describing himself as "a man of the Left," was, with the possible exception of his first play, *Waiting for Lefty*, no innovator where form was concerned. He attempted a poetic realism but it was still trying to represent real people in actual social relationships. And this was perhaps inevitable given his actor's temperament as well as his Marxist commitment; he had the revolutionary's eye on the great public, on the reconstitution of power once a failed capitalism had been brought down— for such was the Marxist and non-Marxist Left position on the proper moral obligation of the artist. But by temperament he was a poet seeking words that would lift him into a takeoff, regardless of his realist political commitments. O'Neill, on the other hand, was not the revolutionary but the rebel with a despairing anarchism in his heart. If he glimpsed any salvation, it was not to arrive in a more benign reconstitution of political power but in the tragic cleansing of the life-lie permanently ensconced in the human condition. Since he took no responsibility in theory for a new and better policy to take the place of the corrupted present one, he was free to explore all sorts of theatrical means by which to set forth the situation of the damned. Moreover, if O'Neill wanted his plays to register, and he surely did, they need not be popular to justify his having written them, for he was hunting the sounding whale of ultimate meaning, and he expected to suffer for it; oppositely, a critical or box-office failure for Odets meant rejection of a very personal kind, a spit in the eye by an ungrateful, self-satisfied bourgeois society. A failed play for Odets was a denial of what he was owed, for he was chasing the public no differently from his bourgeois nonrevolutionary contemporaries. O'Neill could say, and he did, that he was not interested in relations between men, but between Man and God. For America, in his view, was damned and if there were a few individuals who behaved justly and well it was not because they belonged to a particular social class or held a generous or unselfish political viewpoint, but by virtue of a grace whose source is beyond definition.

II

The realism of Broadway—and the Strand and the Boulevard theatre of France—was detested by the would-be poetic dramatists of my generation, just as it had always been since it came into vogue in the nineteenth century. What did this

realism really come down to? A play representing real rather
than symbolic or metaphysical persons and situations, its
main virtue verisimiltude, with no revolutionary implications
for society or even a symbolic statement of some general
truth. Quite simply, conventional realism was conventional
because it implicitly supported the conventions of society,
but it could just as easily do something quite different, or so
it seemed to me. Nevertheless, we thought it the perfect style
for an unchallenging, simpleminded linear middle-class con-
formist view of life. What I found confusing at the time,
however, was that not so very long before, the name
"realism" had been applied to the revolutionary style of
playwrights like Ibsen, Chekhov, and quite frequently
Strindberg, writers whose whole thrust was in opposition to
the bourgeois status quo and the hypocrisies on which it
stood, or, in Chekhov's case, the futilities of the Czarist
system.

My own first playwriting attempt was purely mimetic, a
realistic play about my own family. It won me some prizes
and productions, but, interestingly, I turned at once to a
stylized treatment of life in a gigantic prison, modeled on
Jackson State Penitentiary in Michigan—near Ann Arbor,
where I was in school—the largest prison in the United
States, which I had visited over weekends with a friend who
was its lone psychologist. The theme of that play was that
prisons existed to make desperate workingmen insane. There
was a chorus of sane prisoners chanting from a high overpass
above the stage, and a counter-chorus of the insane trying
to draw the other into their ranks. It was inevitable that I
had to confront the problem of dramatic language, for it was
impossible to engage so vast a human disaster with speech

born in a warm kitchen. I gradually came to wonder if the
essential pressure toward poetic dramatic language—if not of
stylization itself—came from the inclusion of society as a
major element in the play's story or vision. Manifestly, prose
realism was the language of the individual and of private life,
poetry the language of man in crowds, in society. Put another way, prose is the language of family relations; it is the
inclusion of the larger world beyond that naturally opens a
play to the poetic.

But I wanted to succeed, I wanted to emerge and grip an
audience. Minds might be illuminated by speeches thrown
at them but it was by being moved that one was changed.
And so the problem was that our audiences were trained, as
it were, in a pawky realism and were turned off by stylistic
novelty, by "art." How to find a style that would at one and
the same time deeply engage an American audience, which
insisted on a recognizable reality of characters, locales, and
themes, while opening the stage to considerations of public
morality and the mythic social fates—in short, the invisible?

Of course this was not my preoccupation alone. I doubt
there was ever a time when there was so much discussion
about form and style. T. S. Eliot was writing his verse plays,
and Auden and Isherwood theirs; the poetic mimesis of Sean
O'Casey was most popular; and W. B. Yeats's dialogue was
studied if not very often produced. The impulse to poetry
reached into the ex-newspaperman and realistic writer Max-
well Anderson, whose attempts to imitate Elizabethan pros-
ody with contemporary characters and social themes were
widely celebrated, as curios by some, as moving experiences
by others.

To be just to Odets, it was he who challenged the Broadway theatre's addiction to verisimilitude by his idiosyncratic dialogue. And he was surely the first American playwright to be celebrated—and more wildly and lavishly than any other before him—for his writing style. For younger writers such as myself, Odets for a couple of years was the trailblazer; he was bringing the suffering of the Great Depression onto the Broadway stage and making audiences listen. If he had not solved the problem of a contemporary American style, he had dared to invent an often wildly stylized stage speech. But I suppose that since his characters lacked elegance or strangeness, were, in fact, the very exemplars of realistic theatre, Odets was called a realist—indeed, a kind of reporter of Jewish life in the Bronx. I may not have lived in the Bronx but the speech of Brooklyn Jews certainly bore no resemblance to that of Odets's characters.

CARP [in *Golden Boy*]: I'm superdisgusted with you!
 . . . A man hits his wife and it's the first step to
 fascism! Look in the papers! On every side the clouds
 of war! . . . Ask yourself a pertinent remark; could
 a boy make a living playing this instrument [a violin]
 in our competitive civilization today?

ROXY: I think I'll run across the street and pick up an
 eight-cylinder sandwich.

The audiences roared with delight at these inventions. It was as though Odets were trying to turn dialogue into jazz. And his devotees went to his plays especially to pick up his latest deliciously improbable remarks and repeat them to their friends. Had any Bronxite—or anyone else in the

century—really exclaimed, "God's teeth, no!" "What ex-
haust pipe did he crawl out of?" Lorna: "I feel like I'm shot
from a cannon."

Inevitably, in a theatre bounded by realism, this had to be
mistakenly labeled as accurate reportage, news from the
netherworld. But of course it was an invented diction of a
kind never heard before on stage—or off, for that matter.
Odets's fervent ambition was to burst the bounds of Broadway while remaining inside its embrace, and if as time went
on his lines began to seem self-consciously labored, no
longer springing from characters but manifestly from the author and his will-to-poeticize, he at a minimum had made
language the identifying mark of a playwright in America,
and that was something that hadn't happened before.

Admittedly, I did not look at his style with objectivity but
for its potential usefulness in breaking through the con-
stricted realism of our theatre then. Odets was tremendously
exciting to young writers. I was troubled by a tendency in
his plays toward overtheatricalized excess, however—lines
sometimes brought laughter where there should have been
outrage, or pity, or some deeper emotion than amusement
—and at times the plots verged on the schematic. Odets
often overrhapsodized at the climaxes when he should have
been reaching back to ancillary material that was not there.
He wrote terrific scenes, blazing speeches and confrontations
which showed what theatre could be, but with the exception, perhaps, of *Awake and Sing* and the racy *Golden Boy* he
never wrote a play that lifted inexorably to its climactic
revelation.

I came out of the thirties unsure whether there could be
a viable counterform to the realism around me. All I knew

for sure was that a good play must move forward in its depths as rapidly as on its surfaces; word-poetry wasn't enough if there was a fractured poetry in the structure, the gradually revealed illuminating idea behind the whole thing. A real play was the discovery of the unity of its contradictions; the essential poetry was the synthesis of even the least of its parts to form a symbolic meaning. Of course the problem had much to do with language but more primary was how to penetrate my own feelings about myself and the time in which I lived. Ideally, a good play must show as sound an emotional proof of its thesis as a case at law shows factual proof, and you can't do that with words alone, lovely as they might be.

Odets's contribution, ironically, was not his realistic portrayal of society—his alleged aim—but his willingness to be artificial; he brought back artificiality, if you will, just as ten years later Tennessee Williams did with his birdsong from the magnolias. But Williams had an advantage—his language could be far more faithful to its sources in reality. Southern people did love to talk, and in the accents Williams captured (as in *The Glass Menagerie*):

AMANDA: . . . But Laura is, thank heavens, not only pretty but also very domestic. I'm not at all. I never was a bit. I never could make a thing but angel-food cake. Well, in the South we had so many servants. Gone, gone, gone. All vestige of gracious living! Gone completely! I wasn't prepared for what the future brought me. All my gentlemen callers were sons of planters and so of course I assumed that I would be married to one and raise my family on a large piece of land with plenty of servants. But man proposes—and woman accepts the proposal!—To vary that old, old saying a little bit—I married no planter! I married a man who worked for the telephone company! —That gallantly smiling gentleman over there! (*Points to husband's picture.*) A telephone man who—fell in love with long distance! Now he travels and I don't even know where! . . .

This too was called realism, and it probably was in the sense that there were people who talked like this. But then how did it differ from the conventional realistic play? Clearly, it was that the very action of Williams's plays, certainly the best of them, was working toward the building of symbolic meaning that would embrace both the psychological development of his characters and his personal specter of a menacing America struggling with its own sexuality and the anomie born of its dire materialism. In a word, Williams's style arose from his pain and anxiety at being overwhelmed and defeated by a gross violence that underlay the American—one might say the whole Western—ethos.

Their obsession with words notwithstanding, it was their need to communicate their resistance to something death-dealing in the culture that finally pressed Odets and Williams to address the big public and made them playwrights rather than sequestered poets. Stylistic invention without an implicit commitment of some kind to a more humane vision of life is a boat without rudder or cargo or destination—or worse, it is the occupation of the dilettante. Odets, when he began, thought his egalitarian Marxism would heal America and create its new community, but that ideology devolved into a rote religion before the thirties had even passed. Williams unfurled the banner of a forlorn but resisting heroism to the violence against the oddball, the poet, the sexual dissident. But it may as well be admitted that in their different ways both men in the end unwittingly collaborated with the monster they saw as trying to destroy them.

The plays these men wrote were shields raised against the many-arrowed darkness, but in the end there was little from outside to give them the spiritual support to complete their creative lives. Odets's best work ended with his rejection by Broadway and his move to Hollywood; Williams, likewise rejected, kept nevertheless to his trade, experimenting with forms and new methods that drew no encouragement from reviewers unable or unwilling to notice that the theatre culture had boxed in a writer of greatness who was struggling to find an audience in the passing crowd of a generation other than his own. At his strongest he had spoken for and to the center of society, in a style it could relate to, an enhanced, visionary realism. In the end a writer has no one to blame for his failings, not even himself, but the brutally dismissive glee of critics toward Williams's last plays simply laid more sticks on his burden. Toward the end he was still outside, scratching on the glass, as he had once put it, and it was the shadowed edges of life that drew him, the borderland where how things are said is everything, and everything has been said before.

The advent of the Absurd and of Beckett and his followers both obscured and illuminated the traditional elements of the discussion of theatre style. For O'Neill a good style was basically a question of the apt use of metaphor and argot. "God, if I could write like that!" he wrote to O'Casey, who, incidentally, would no doubt have labeled himself a realistic writer in the sense that he was giving his audiences the substance of their life conficts. But like Williams, O'Casey came from a culture which loved talk and sucked on language like a sweet candy.

MRS. GROGAN: Oh, you've got a cold on you, Fluther.

FLUTHER: Oh, it's only a little one.

MRS. GROGAN: You'd want to be careful, all th' same. I knew a woman, a big lump of a woman, red-faced and round-bodied, a little awkward on her feet; you'd think, to look at her, she could put out her two arms an' lift a two-storied house on th' top of her head; got a ticklin' in her throat, an' a little cough, an' th' next mornin' she had a little catchin' in her chest, an' they had just time to wet her lips with a little rum, an' off she went.

(Juno and the Paycock)

Even in the most mundane of conversational exchanges O'Casey sought, and as often as not found, the lift of poetry. Indeed, that was the whole point—that the significantly poetic sprang from the raw and real experience of ordinary people. J. M. Synge, O'Casey's forerunner at the turn of the century, had struck a similar chord; Synge was in a supremely conscious revolt against the banality of most theatre language. As John Gassner noted, in Ireland the popular imagination was still, according to Synge, "fiery and magnificent, and tender; so that those of us who wish to write start with a chance that is not given to writers in places where the springtime of local life has been forgotten, and the harvest is a memory only, and the straw has been turned into bricks."

Synge rejected the then-dominant Ibsen and Zola for the "joyless and pallid words" of their realism and as in *Riders to the Sea*, when the women are lamenting the deaths of so many of their men working the angry sea:

> MAURYA : In the big world the old people do be leaving things after them for their sons and children, but in this place it is the young men do be leaving things behind for them that do be old.

As far as style is concerned, the Beckett difference, as it might be called, was to introduce humble people—bums, in fact, or social sufferers—with the plainest of language, but arranged so as to announce and develop pure theme. His could be called a presentational thematic play, announcing what it was about and never straying very far from what it was conceived of to prove, or what his instinct had led him to confirm. Beckett had parted with inferential playwriting, where speeches inferred the author's thematic intentions while hewing to an apparently autonomous story building to a revelatory climax that united story and theme. In Beckett the story *was* the theme, inseparably so. Moreover, as will be shown in a moment, he interpreted the theme himself in his dialogue.

If—instead of the prewar poetic drama's requirement of an elevated tone or diction—the most common speech was now prized, it was not the speech of realistic plays. It was a speech skewed almost out of recognition by a surreal commitment to what at first had seemed to be the impotence of human hopes, and hence the futility of action itself. All but the flimsiest connections between speeches were eliminated, creating an atmosphere of sinister danger (in Pinter) or immanence (in Beckett). It was quite as though the emphatic absence of purpose in the characters had created a loss of syntax. It seems that in later years Beckett took pains to clarify this impression of human futility, emphasizing the struggle *against* inertia as his theme. In any case, however ridiculous so much of his dialogue exchanges are, the tenderness of feeling in his work is emphatically not that of the cynic or the hard ironist.

The dominating theme of *Godot* is stasis and the struggle to overcome humanity's endlessly repetitious paralysis before the need to act and change. We hear it plainly and stripped clean of plot or even incident.

ESTRAGON: Then adieu.

POZZO: Adieu.

VLADIMIR: Adieu.

POZZO: Adieu.

Silence. No one moves.

VLADIMIR: Adieu.

POZZO: Adieu.

ESTRAGON: Adieu.

Silence.

POZZO: And thank you.

VLADIMIR: Thank *you.*

POZZO: Not at all.

ESTRAGON: Yes yes.

POZZO: No no.

VLADIMIR: Yes yes.

ESTRAGON: No no.

Silence.

POZZO: I don't seem to be able . . . (*long hesitation*)
. . . to depart.

ESTRAGON: Such is life.

This is a vaudeville at the edge of the cliff, but vaudeville anyway, so I may be forgiven for being reminded of Jimmy Durante's ditty—"Didja ever get the feelin' that you wanted to go? But still you had the feelin' that you wanted to stay?"

It is a language shorn of metaphor, simile, everything but its instructions, so to speak. The listener hears the theme like a nail drawn across a pane of glass.

So the struggle with what might be called reportorial realism, written "the way people talk," is at least as old as the century. As for myself, my own tendency has been to shift styles according to the nature of my subject. *All My Sons, The Crucible, A View from the Bridge, Death of a Salesman, The Price, The American Clock,* my earliest work, like *The Golden Years,* about the destruction of Mexico by the Spaniards, and the more recent plays, like *The Creation of the World, Some Kind of Love Story,* and *The Last Yankee,* differ very much in their language. This, in order to find speech that springs naturally out of the characters and their backgrounds rather than imposing a general style. If my approach to playwriting is partly literary, I hope it is well hidden. Leroy Hamilton is a native New England carpenter and speaks like one, and not like the New York working men and women in *A Memory of Two Mondays*, or Eddie Carbone, who comes out of a quite different culture.

So the embrace of something called realism is obviously very wide; it can span the distance between a Turgenev and a Becque, between Wedekind and your latest Broadway hit. The main thing I sought in *The Last Yankee* was to make real my sense of the life of such people, the kind of man swinging the hammer through a lifetime, the kind of woman waiting forever for her ship to come in. And second, my view of their present confusion and, if you will, decay and possible recovery. They are bedrock, aspiring not to greatness but to other gratifications—successful parenthood, decent children and a decent house and a decent car and an occasional nice evening with family or friends, and above all, of course, some financial security. Needless to say, they are people who can be inspired to great and noble sacrifice, but also to bitter hatreds. As the world goes I suppose they are the luckiest people, but some of them—a great many, in fact—have grown ill with what would once have been called a sickness of the soul.

And that is the subject of the play, its "matter." For depression is far from being merely a question of an individual's illness, although it appears as that, of course; it is at the same time, most especially in Patricia Hamilton's case, the grip on her of a success mythology which is both naïve and brutal, and which, to her misfortune, she has made her own. And opposing it, quite simply, is her husband Leroy's incredibly enduring love for her, for nature and the world.

A conventionally realistic play would no doubt have attempted to create a "just-like-life" effect, with the sickness gradually rising out of the normal routines of the family's life, and calling up our empathy by virtue of our instant identification with familiar reality. But while Patricia Hamilton, the carpenter's wife, is seen as an individual sufferer, the context of her illness is equally important because, for one thing, she knows, as do many such patients, that more Americans (and West Europeans) are in hospitals for depression than for any other ailment. In life, with such people, a high degree of objectification or distancing exists, and the style of the play had to reflect the fact that they commonly know a great deal about the social setting of the illness even as they are unable to tear themselves free of it. And this affects the play's style.

It opens by directly, even crudely, grasping the core of its central preoccupation—the moral and social myths feeding the disease; and we have a discussion of the hospital's enormous parking lot, a conversation bordering on the absurd. I would call this realism, but it is far from the tape-recorded kind. Frick, like Leroy Hamilton, has arrived for a visit with his wife, and after a moment's silence while the two strangers grope for a conversational opening . . .

FRICK: Tremendous parking space down there. 'They need that for?

LEROY: Well a lot of people visit on weekends. Fills up pretty much.

FRICK: Really? That whole area?

LEROY: Pretty much.

FRICK: 'Doubt that.

The play is made of such direct blows aimed at the thematic center; there is a vast parking space because crowds of stricken citizens converge on this place to visit mothers, fathers, brothers, and sisters. So that the two patients we may be about to meet are not at all unique. This is in accord with the vision of the play, which is intended to be both close up and wide, psychological and social, subjective and objective, and manifestly so. To be sure, there is a realistic tone to this exchange—people do indeed seem to talk this way—but an inch below is the thematic selectivity which drives the whole tale. Perhaps it needs to be said that this split vision has informed all the plays I have written. I have tried to make things seen in their social context and simultaneously felt as intimate testimony, and that requires a style, but one that draws as little attention to itself as possible, for I would wish a play to be absorbed rather than merely observed.

I have called this play a comedy, a comedy about a tragedy, and I am frankly not sure why. Possibly it is due to the absurdity of people constantly comparing themselves to others—something we all do to one degree or another, but in Patricia's case to the point of illness.

PATRICIA: There was something else you said. About standing on line.

LEROY: On line?

PATRICIA: That you'll always be at the head of the line
because . . . *breaks off.*

LEROY: I'm the only one on it. . . . We're really all on
a one-person line, Pat. I learned that in these years.

The play's language, then, has a surface of everyday realism, but its action is overtly stylized rather than "natural."

Finally, a conventionally realistic work about mental illness would be bound to drive to a reverberating climax. But
repression is the cultural inheritance of these New England-
ers and such theatricality would be a betrayal of *their* style of
living and dying. Indeed, short of suicide, the illness, prop-
erly speaking, never ends in the sense of tying all the loose
strings, nor should the play, which simply sets the boundaries
of the possible. For the theme is hope rather than completion
or achievement, and hope is tentative always.

A play about them should have a certain amplitude of
sound, nothing greater or less, reflecting their tight yet often
deeply felt culture. And in a play about them they should
recognize themselves—and even possibly what drives them
mad—just like the longshoremen who saw themselves in *A
View from the Bridge* or the cops in *The Price* or the salespeople
in *Death of a Salesman*. That would be a satisfactory realism
as I saw it.

I suppose the form itself of *The Last Yankee* is as astrin-
gently direct and uncluttered as it is because these people
are supremely the prey of the culture, if only because it is
never far from the center of their minds—the latest film or
TV show, the economy's ups and downs, and above all the

endless advertising-encouraged self-comparisons with others who are more or less successful than they. This ritualistic preoccupation is at the play's dramatic core and, I felt, ought not be unclear or misted over, for it is from its grip they must be freed if they are ever to be free at all. Hence, the repeated references to ambition, to success and failure, to wealth and poverty, to economic survival, to the kind of car one drives and the suit one wears. In a word, the play could not be amorphously "realistic" if it was to reflect the obsessiveness of the characters in life. So if *The Last Yankee* is realism it is of this kind resulting from an intense selectivity, which in turn is derived from the way these people live and feel.

But obviously, to make such a strictly thematic play demands intense condensation and the syncopating of idea and feeling and language. More than one actor in my plays has told me that it is surprisingly difficult to memorize the dialogue. It sounds like real, almost like reported talk, when in fact it is intensely composed, compressed, "angled" into an inevitability that seems natural but isn't. For it is always necessary to employ the artificial in order arrive at the real. So that the question I bring to a play is not whether its form and style are new or old, experimental or traditional, but first, whether it brings news, something truly felt by its author, something thought through to its conclusion and its significance; and second, whether its form is beautiful, or wasteful, whether it is aberrant for aberrancy's sake, full of surprises that discover little, and so on.

Something called Realism can land us further from common reality than the most fantastic caprice. But in the end, if stylization in theatre needs justification—and it does, of course—it is not in its novelty but in its enhancement of discovery of how life works in our time. How a thing is said is therefore only as important as what it is saying. The proof is the deep pile of experimental plays of two, three, five, ten years ago, which can be appreciated now only by the scholar-specialist, a pile, incidentally, no smaller than the one for so many realistic plays of the same era. So finding the truth is no easier now when we are totally free to use any stylistic means at hand than it was a century or half a century ago when a play had to be "real" to even be read, and had to make sense to sensible people.

Call it a question of personal taste rather than principle, but I think that in theatre work there is an optimum balance between two kinds of approaches. One is the traditional attempt to fill characters with acknowledged emotion, "as in life." The other is, in effect, to evacuate emotion from characters and merely refer to it rather than acting it out. Brecht, for one, tried to do this and failed, excepting in his most agitprop and forgettable plays. Actually, the strict containment not of emotion but of emotionalism is the hallmark of the Greek tragic plays, of Molière and Racine and the Japanese No plays, while Shakespeare, it seems to me, is the balance, the fusion of idea and feeling. In short, it is by no means the abstracting of emotion I dislike; on the contrary, it is the lack of it and the substitution for it of fashionably alienated ironies.

As I am not a critic and would not do anything to make any writer's life harder, I will desist from naming names, but there has been a plethora of plays in recent years whose claim to modernity is based on indicated rather than felt emotion, on the assumption, I suppose, that this *sec* quality intellectualizes a work and saves it from the banality associated with writing aimed at the audience's belly rather than at its head. The devil to be avoided is, of course, sentimentality—emotion unearned. But emotion can be earned, of course. Yet a play that is not camp and moves people is in danger of dismissal. (Unless it appears in old films, which we allow ourselves to be moved by if at the same instant we can protect our modernity by feeling superior to their time-bound naïveté.) But if the pun can be pardoned, man lives not by head alone, and the balance between the two modes, one aimed at the mind and one at the flesh, as it were, is what will interpret life more fully, rather than headline it with conceptualizations that too often simply clump about on the stilts of dry irony that time and the shifts of cultural politics will make thoroughly disposable. After all, at least part of the aim of a modern play must be to show what life now *feels alike.*

Ultimately every assault on the human mystery falls back to the ground, changing little, but the flight of the arrow continues claiming our attention over more time when its direction is toward the castle rather than the wayward air.

FOR THE BEST IN PAPERBACKS, LOOK FOR THE ⓟ

In every corner of the world, on every subject under the sun, Penguin represents quality and variety—the very best in publishing today.

For complete information about books available from Penguin—including Pelicans, Puffins, Peregrines, and Penguin Classics—and how to order them, write to us at the appropriate address below. Please note that for copyright reasons the selection of books varies from country to country.

In the United Kingdom: For a complete list of books available from Penguin in the U.K., please write to *Dept E.P., Penguin Books Ltd, Harmondsworth, Middlesex, UB7 0DA.*

In the United States: For a complete list of books available from Penguin in the U.S., please write to *Consumer Sales, Penguin USA, P.O. Box 999—Dept. 17109, Bergenfield, New Jersey 07621-0120.* VISA and MasterCard holders call 1-800-253-6476 to order all Penguin titles.

In Canada: For a complete list of books available from Penguin in Canada, please write to *Penguin Books Canada Ltd, 10 Alcorn Avenue, Suite 300, Toronto, Ontario, Canada M4V 3B2.*

In Australia: For a complete list of books available from Penguin in Australia, please write to the *Marketing Department, Penguin Books Ltd, P.O. Box 257, Ringwood, Victoria 3134.*

In New Zealand: For a complete list of books available from Penguin in New Zealand, please write to the *Marketing Department, Penguin Books (NZ) Ltd, Private Bag, Takapuna, Auckland 9.*

In India: For a complete list of books available from Penguin, please write to *Penguin Overseas Ltd, 706 Eros Apartments, 56 Nehru Place, New Delhi, 110019.*

In Holland: For a complete list of books available from Penguin in Holland, please write to *Penguin Books Nederland B.V., Postbus 195, NL-1380AD Weesp, Netherlands.*

In Germany: For a complete list of books available from Penguin, please write to *Penguin Books Ltd, Friedrichstrasse 10-12, D-6000 Frankfurt Main 1, Federal Republic of Germany.*

In Spain: For a complete list of books available from Penguin in Spain, please write to *Longman, Penguin España, Calle San Nicolas 15, E-28013 Madrid, Spain.*

In Japan: For a complete list of books available from Penguin in Japan, please write to *Longman Penguin Japan Co Ltd, Yamaguchi Building, 2-12-9 Kanda Jimbocho, Chiyoda-Ku, Tokyo 101, Japan.*

☐ **"MASTER HAROLD"** . . . **AND THE BOYS**
   Athol Fugard

A stunning exploration of apartheid and racism, *"Master Harold"* . . . *and the boys* "is beyond beauty." (Frank Rich, *The New York Times*)
                    60 pages   ISBN: 0-14-048187-7

☐ **CONTEMPORARY SCENES FOR STUDENT ACTORS**
   Edited by Michael Schulman and Eva Mekler

Containing more than 80 scenes by major modern playwrights, *Contemporary Scenes for Student Actors* includes dialogues for two men, two women, and one man and one woman.

                    438 pages   ISBN: 0-14-048153-2